Pedro
The Puerto Rican Parrot

LOVE can change the World

WILDLIFE
VETS
INTERNATIONAL

All author royalties from the sale
of this book will go to WVI.
www.wildlifevetsinternational.org

This book is dedicated to Lucy, Eithne and Ailsa
and our wonderful Home Grown family.
~ B J

This book is for Shreya.
~ S C

First published in Great Britain in 2021
by Little Steps Publishing
Uncommon, 126 New King's Rd, London SW6 4LZ
www.littlestepspublishing.co.uk

ISBN: 978-1-912678-38-9

Designed by Verity Clark

Printed in China
3 5 7 9 10 8 6 4 2

MIX
Paper from
responsible sources
FSC
www.fsc.org   FSC® C130668

LOVE can change the World

Pedro
The Puerto Rican Parrot

Beverly Jatwani   Sunita Chawdhary

Little Steps
PUBLISHING

Mr Gonzales was the owner of the local animal rescue centre. He liked to start his mornings going through his paperwork while sipping a hot cup of coffee in peace and quiet. But on this Saturday morning, things were anything but quiet!

The noise seemed to come from the front door. So he grabbed his keys, opened the creaky door and gasped.

SQUAWK
SQUAWK
SQUAWK

please look after me

Right before his eyes was a noisy green parrot.
It was obvious that the bird was hurt. 'Don't worry, little one,' said Mr Gonzales, picking it up. 'You're safe now.'

DING went the shop's doorbell as Dominic and his mum
stepped in. 'Buenos días, Mr Gonzales,' they said.
But all they heard was…

'GOOD MORNING!'
shouted Mr Gonzales to them.
'HOW CAN I HELP YOU?'

'We brought some food for the shelter,' Dominic's
mum replied. 'But where is that noise coming from?'

'Ah, that would be Pedro,' said Mr Gonzales,
'a Puerto Rican parrot that was abandoned
this morning. Its wing is badly injured.'

SQUAWK
SQUAWK
SQUAWK

Dominic's eyebrows shot up. 'A Puerto Rican parrot?
We just learned about them at school! They are some
of the most endangered birds on our planet.'

He followed the noise and
spotted the emerald-green parrot.

'Wow!' he said. 'Can we take
him home, Mama? Please?'

His mum shook her head. 'I'm sorry, Dominic, but the bird is badly injured...'

SQUAWK SQUAWK

'It will need constant care...'

SQUAWK SQUAWK

'We don't have a place for it, and...'

SQUAWK

'It's far too noisy!'

SQUAWK

Dominic shed a tear with disappointment.
'Maybe you can come and visit him?'
suggested Mr Gonzales. 'We're always
on the lookout for helpers here
at the rescue centre.'

Dominic looked at his mum,
who smiled and gave him a nod.

'Yes!' cried Dominic.
'I'd love to help.'

'Fantastic!' replied Mr Gonzales. 'You'll be in charge of Pedro. You'll have to feed him every day and change his bandages once a week until his wing heals. But, most of all,' he added, 'make sure to give him plenty of LOVE.'

'LOVE?' asked Dominic.
'Yes,' replied Mr Gonzales, with a knowing look, 'love will make the difference.'
He thanked Dominic and his mum for their donations. 'See you tomorrow, Dominic,' he said as they left.

The following day, Dominic arrived at the centre, bright and early.
Pedro's squawks could be heard from the car park.
Dominic greeted Mr Gonzales, who looked like he was suffering
from a bad headache, and headed towards the aviary.

SQUAWK
SQUAWK
SQUAWK

At the sight of Dominic, Pedro started squawking even louder, flapping his good wing. He looked very scared. Dominic's attempts to get close were met by deafening noises and feathers flying about.

He didn't know what to do, but he was sure of one thing. 'I will not give up on you,' he said, looking into Pedro's white-rimmed eyes. Suddenly, Mr Gonzales's words came back to him: Love will make the difference.

Holding some seeds in the palm of his hand, Dominic
gently opened the cage. He whispered soothing words
and Pedro seemed to stop and listen.

'Calm down, Pedro. I'm your friend.'

The bird hesitated at first, but then he got closer and started pecking at the seeds. Dominic gently stroked Pedro's feathers as he ate. As Pedro cooed and chirped, Dominic felt deliriously happy.

After a week, Dominic changed Pedro's bandage,
being careful not to make it too tight.

Every day, Dominic fed Pedro and
talked softly to him. He enjoyed telling
Pedro about his day.
Visiting his friend at the rescue centre
was Dominic's favourite part of the day.
He'd rush there after school and head
straight to his cage.

But on one rainy Monday afternoon, Dominic found Pedro's cage was empty. He ran to Mr Gonzales. 'Where is Pedro?' he asked in distress. 'I'm sorry,' Mr Gonzales replied, 'but he's been adopted. A lovely family came to pick him up this morning. They'll look after him until he's ready to be released back into the wild.'

Dominic's heart ached. He was so sad that he didn't even get a chance to say goodbye, he thought as he walked back home.

But as soon as he opened his front door, shouting, 'Mama,
I'm home!', he heard a familiar sound echoing through the air.

SQUAWK

SQUAWK

SQUAWK

'Pedro!' exclaimed Dominic,
as he ran towards his best friend.

'You did such an amazing job looking after him that we decided to bring him home,' said his mum. 'Thank you,' cried Dominic, filled with happiness.

Home Sweet Home

Dominic and Pedro became inseparable. Dominic let the bird perch
on his bed and would fall asleep to Pedro's melodic whistling.

A few days went by until it was time again for Dominic to change the bird's bandage.

But before he could put on the new one, Pedro began to flap his wing!

Pedro!' said Dominic happily. 'You can fly again! 'Although this means that it's time for you to go home. I'd love to keep you, but you belong in the rainforest.'

I LOVE YOU!

The drive to the parrot recovery program in El Yunque National Forest was a long and quiet one. 'I'm going to miss you, Pedro,' sighed Dominic. 'Take care of yourself. I will do everything I can to protect you and all the other Puerto Rican parrots.'

He petted the top of Pedro's head. 'I love you, my friend.' 'I love you,' mimicked the bird.

Dominic's heart pounded. 'You spoke!'
Pedro spread his striking green and blue wings and soared
into the sky. Dominic wiped a happy tear from his eye.

That night, Dominic was restless and couldn't sleep.
As he turned over in bed, his hand brushed against
something on his pillow.

It looked like a piece of a puzzle.

'What? How?' he muttered.

On the puzzle piece was the word LOVE.

Dominic held it tight. He somehow knew it was a gift from
Pedro and that, one day, he would see his friend again.

Facts about Puerto Rican parrots

- Puerto Rican parrots are one of the rarest birds on Earth.
- There are only around 600* of them left in the wild and in breeding programmes.
- They live in the tree canopy in the rainforests of Puerto Rico.
- The parrots are emerald green in colour, have a red forehead and wide, white eye rings.
- They eat mainly fruit, leaves, bark, flowers and seeds.
- Male and female Puerto Rican parrots look alike.
- Loss of habitat by deforestation is the main reason they have become endangered.

* Numbers may vary.